SPORTS STAR CHAMPIONS

CRISTIANO RONALDO

Champion Soccer Star

John A. Torres

Enslow Publishing
101 W. 23rd Street
Suite 240
New York, NY 10011
USA

enslow.com

Published in 2018 by Enslow Publishing, LLC.
101 W. 23rd Street, Suite 240, New York, NY 10011

Library of Congress Cataloging-in-Publication Data

Names: Torres, John Albert, author.
Title: Cristiano Ronaldo : champion soccer star / John Torres.
Description: New York, NY : Enslow Publishing, 2018. | Series: Sports Star Champions | Includes bibliographical references and index. | Audience: Grade 6-8.
Identifiers: LCCN 2017003132| ISBN 9780766086883 (library-bound) | ISBN 9780766087552 (pbk.) | ISBN 9780766087569 (6-pack)
Subjects: LCSH: Ronaldo, Cristiano, 1985- —Juvenile literature. | Soccer players—Portugal—Biography—Juvenile literature.
Classification: LCC GV942.7.R626 T66 2018 | DDC 796.334092 [B] —dc23
LC record available at https://lccn.loc.gov/2017003132

Printed in the United States of America

To Our Readers: We have done our best to make sure all websites in this book were active and appropriate when we went to press. However, the author and the publisher have no control over and assume no liability for the material available on those websites or on any websites they may link to. Any comments or suggestions can be sent by email to customerservice@enslow.com.

Photo Credits: Cover, p. 1 fotopress/Getty Images; pp. 4-5 Dan Mullan/Getty Images; pp. 6-7, 36 Matthias Hangst/Getty Images; p. 9 Peter Hermes Furian/Shutterstock.com; p. 11 Gregorio Cunha/AFP/Getty Images; p. 15 Octavio Passos/Getty Images; pp. 17, 21, 30 AFP/Getty Images; p. 20 John Peters/Manchester United/Getty Images; p. 23 Adrian Dennis/AFP/Getty Images; p. 25 Michael Steele/Getty Images; p. 27 Yuri Cortez/AFP/Getty Images; p. 28 Jasper Juinen/Getty Images; p. 33 Francisco Leong/AFP/Getty Images; p. 34 Adam Pretty/Getty Images; pp. 38, 43 Denis Doyle/Getty Images; p. 39 Getty images; p. 41 Ian Gavan/Getty Images.

Contents

Introduction:
Champion Teammate

What is it that makes a champion? Is it hard work, determination, natural talent, intelligence, or sheer will? It's probably a combination of all of those things. It is also how someone reacts to adversity—what he or she does when things don't go right. That could not be truer than in the case of legendary soccer superstar Cristiano Ronaldo, arguably the best player in the world.

The tackle came in hard and fast. Ronaldo crumbled to the ground. He knew something was wrong right away. It was his knee. It was very early in the 2016 Euro league championship match. Ronaldo had led his country's national team, Portugal, to improbable victories in the early rounds. Now here were Ronaldo and his teammates on the verge of pulling off a major soccer upset. Only the mighty national team from France stood in their way.

Play was stopped as the great Ronaldo had to be helped to the sidelines. The trainers wrapped his knee after he insisted that he wanted to continue playing through the knee injury. But it soon became clear that this important match would have to be decided without him. Twice during the first half of the match, Ronaldo fell to the ground in agony. He clutched his knee and cried tears of anguish.

Not only was he in excruciating pain but he did not want to let his teammates down. As he left the field of play for the third and final time, Ronaldo felt as if his championship hopes had been crushed. It was the most important match of his career, and he would not be able to play for the second half.

His teammates were unsure of what to expect. No one believed they would be able to beat France without their best player leading the way. But then something happened. Ronaldo knew that he would still be able to help his teammates. If he couldn't score goals maybe there was something else he could do.

Cristiano Ronaldo grimaces in pain after injuring his knee during the 2016 Euro league championship match.

He left the trainer's room and joined his team in the locker room at halftime. He implored them not to give up and to keep challenging for every loose ball. He told them they had the talent and the tenacity to beat France.

"Cristiano had fantastic words for us," said teammate Cédric Soares. "He gave us a lot of confidence and said 'listen people, I'm sure we will win, so stay together and fight for it.' … he was fantastic. His attitude was unbelievable. He always had a lot of motivational words and all the team of course reacted to them, so it was very good."

That wasn't all. Ronaldo limped up and down the sideline for the entire second half of the championship game encouraging his team to keep fighting and playing hard. He was like a second coach for the team.

When it was over, Portugal had accomplished the improbable. No one thought they could beat France, especially without Cristiano Ronaldo. His teammates praised him and credited him with the victory. Seconds after the referee blew the final whistle, Ronaldo was mobbed by his teammates as he raised the championship trophy. He cried once more, but this time they were tears of joy.

After inspiring his teammates to victory, Ronaldo proudly hoists the European championship trophy.

1

From Crybaby to Little Bee

Cristiano Ronaldo dos Santos Aveiro was the fourth and youngest child born to Maria Dolores dos Santos, a cook, and her husband, José Dinis Aveiro, a gardener. He came into the world on February 5, 1985, on an island off the coast of the European country of Portugal.

The Portuguese island of Madeira, off the west coast of the country, is a popular vacation area with lush and gorgeous flowers and beautiful beaches. The island has wealthy residents who live in large mansions.

But there are poor neighborhoods, too, and Ronaldo grew up in the very poor mountain neighborhood of San Antonio. The family's home had a tin roof, but it had a view of the ocean. Cristiano would sometimes sit and admire the beauty.

Life was hard for the family but grew even tougher as Dinis, Cristiano's father, battled the disease of alcoholism. His drinking grew worse and worse, and he had a difficult time keeping a job. He bounced from one position to another. Cristiano's mother often worked a second job cleaning houses to be able to afford food for her children.

Because he was so often out of work, Cristiano's father spent a lot of time volunteering. Then he worked part-time as the equipment manager for a local professional soccer club, Andorinha. In Europe, many towns have their own soccer club where there are different levels of play—from young children to grown men getting paid to play.

Cristiano Ronaldo grew up on the Portuguese island of Madeira.

UP CLOSE

Cristiano Ronaldo was named after US president Ronald Reagan, who had been a Hollywood movie star before going into politics.

While he was there, Dinis became friends with former soccer star Fernao Barros Sousa, who was now playing out the end of his career at Andorinha. He asked Sousa to become Cristiano's godfather. This was beyond symbolic. Dinis wanted to make sure his son would have a strong guiding force in his life in case anything were to happen to him. But it also meant that Sousa would take a very active role in young Cristiano's life, almost as if he were a second father.

That connection helped cultivate one of the best soccer stars of all times, as Cristiano would almost always accompany his father to the soccer fields while he worked. He watched the men play and dreamed of one day being out there.

Even before he was old enough to dream about being a soccer star, he would play on the patio of his small home. When he was only two years old, he was kicking a soccer ball. There was just something about that ball and his foot that seemed connected. As he grew older and spent more and more time with his father and godfather at the soccer fields, it became pretty clear that the young boy had some natural talent.

"When he was little, he was just like other kids," Sousa told a soccer magazine years later. "But he had something that was different from the others and that was that he played a lot of (soccer). Even from a young age. When the other kids were studying, he put his studies on the back seat in order to play football."

That natural talent became an obsession that didn't always make his mother happy. He skipped chores to play soccer, and he often skipped his homework and schoolwork to play and watch soccer. He saw how the older players trained, practiced, and played, and he tried to copy them as best as he could. It paid off. By the time he was eight years old, Cristiano tried out for the Andorinha youth club and easily made the team.

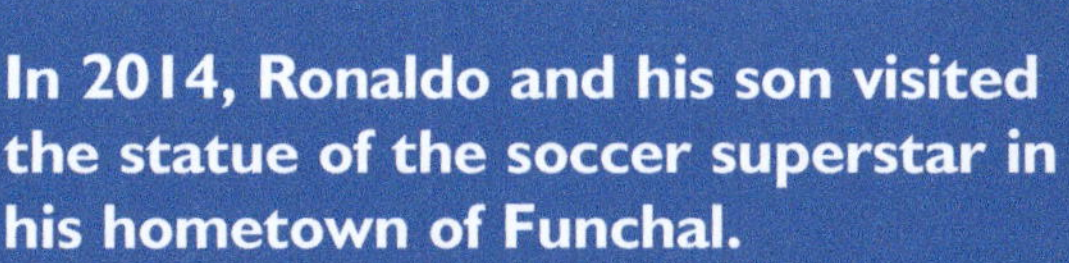

In 2014, Ronaldo and his son visited the statue of the soccer superstar in his hometown of Funchal.

Soccer, er, Futbol?

Soccer is by far the most popular sport in Europe and South America. Americans call the sport "soccer." Other English-speaking countries refer to the sport as "football," and Spanish-speaking countries say "futbol."

No one is really 100 percent sure who invented the game, though many believe a variation of soccer was first played in China about two thousand years ago. Others claim it was originated by the ancient Greeks or the ancient Romans. The one thing many can agree on is that the modern-day game of soccer, the way we know it today, was perfected in England.

"All he wanted to do as a boy was play football [soccer]," said his godfather, Fernao Sousa. "He loved the game so much he'd miss meals or escape out of his bedroom window with a ball when he was supposed to be doing his homework."

Even when he was told by his schoolteachers to leave his soccer ball at home, Cristiano would make one out of socks during recess in order to play the game with his friends.

"He would always find a way of playing football in the playground," his mother said. "I don't know how he managed it."

Cristiano's passion for soccer, for winning, and for playing well was so intense that he often cried if he did not get the ball, if his teammates argued, or if his team lost. Because of this his teammates gave him the nickname "Crybaby."

But by the time he turned ten, Cristiano had already earned another nickname: "Little Bee." That was because he was so fast and tenacious on the field that it was as if he were buzzing around like a bee.

One of his youth coaches remembers that he was so good as a ten-year-old that he was already the best player. His passing was sharp. His goal-scoring kicks were fantastic. His defense was unstoppable. He had it all. He was an all-around great player, and he seemed to have a vision of the field that no one else had. He could see the play and the field unfolding before him like the much older players were able to do.

In one game he scored three goals by halftime, and his team was winning 3–0. But he got injured and could not play in the second half. His team lost 4–3.

He was a phenom, a young player who was so much better than the other kids his age. It wasn't long before other clubs around the Portuguese island of Madeira, including the biggest and most popular—Nacional—started taking notice of this busy little bee on the soccer field who couldn't be stopped.

With the right training and guidance, he would only get better. And Sousa, his godfather, would once again play a pivotal role.

2 Getting Noticed

Cristiano Ronaldo's godfather, Fernao Sousa, helped introduce him to the sport of soccer. He was a pro player, and the boy looked up to him. He was also supportive of the very young Cristiano learning how to play. Sometimes he was even like a second father.

But Sousa had gone to work as a scout for the best team in the country—Nacional—by the time Cristiano was eight years old. He had no idea that the boy had become so good at soccer.

As a scout, Sousa's job was to go around the country and find young players with exceptional soccer skills and sign them up for the Nacional Academy. This is not unusual. For example, one of the world's best players, Lionel Messi, left Argentina at the age of twelve after signing a contract to attend the FC Barcelona Academy. He has been there ever since and has been a star for Barcelona for many years.

There was so much buzz about a ten-year-old playing soccer back in Sousa's hometown of Andorinha that the Nacional club sent him there to check the player out. He noted that the boy was faster and stronger than all the other players on the field. He also noted that he had a very strong kick and had a knack for scoring goals.

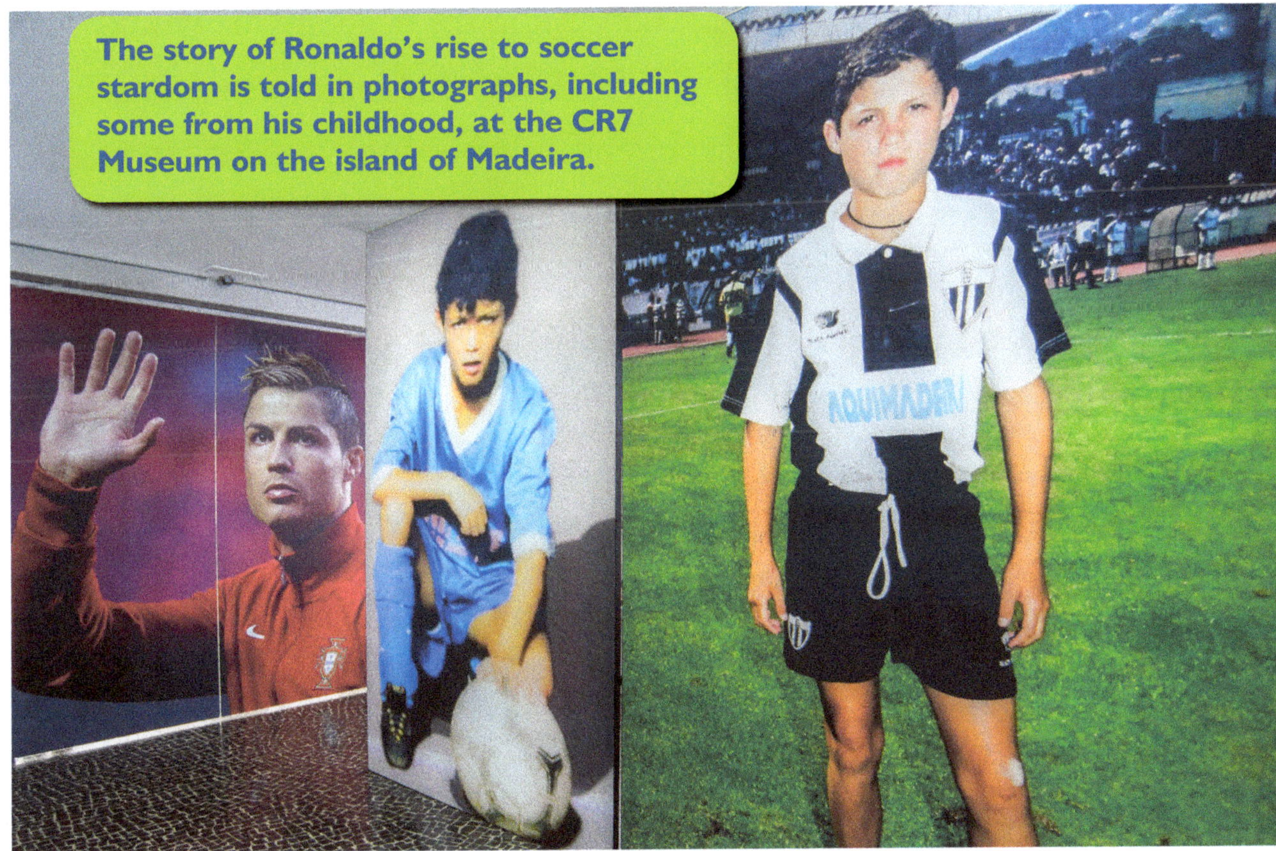

The story of Ronaldo's rise to soccer stardom is told in photographs, including some from his childhood, at the CR7 Museum on the island of Madeira.

When Sousa realized who it was, he couldn't believe his own eyes.

"I went there to see Andorinha play and I realized that the boy was Ronaldo!" he would later tell a soccer magazine. "I was interested in taking him to Nacional to come and play soccer."

But first, Sousa had to convince Cristiano's mother, Dolores. She was very supportive of soccer but was worried because Cristiano wasn't taking his schooling seriously. She wanted to be assured that if he went to the academy he would be attending classes. But she also knew that her son had a talent that is rarely seen. She agreed, and her son's soccer career started taking shape.

When Cristiano arrived at Nacional Futbol Club, he was surprised to learn that just about everyone had already heard of him. He was only ten years old, but he already had a great reputation.

"His talent was known," his Nacional youth coach, Pedro Talinhas, would say. "The scouts and the people working at the clubs considered him the best youngster in Madeira. He was still young at that time, but they could see he had something special."

ESCOLAS

REGIONAL

ÉPOCA

94-95

ASSOCIAÇÃO DE FUTEBOL DO FUNCHAL

A.F.F.

NOME CRISTIANO RONALDO DOS SANTOS AVEIRO

CLUBE Clube Futebol Andorinha

LICENÇA N.º

17.182

O SECRETÁRIO GERAL

This was Cristiano Ronaldo's soccer identification card when he played for the Andorinha Football Club from 1994–1995.

One of the things that set Cristiano apart from the other players his age at the academy was that he was adept at using both feet. He could shoot and pass just as well with his right foot as with his left. He also had a skill for creating spectacular goals. His coach described his goals as something beautiful to watch.

Because he was so good at Nacional, Cristiano was moved up to play a higher level against boys who were older than he was and already teenagers. Then something unheard of happened. The coach made Cristiano the captain of the team! It was the first time the youngest player on the squad was given such an important role. The captain helps lead practice and has to serve as a role model for the rest of his teammates. He continued training hard and impressing his coaches and the other players. Whatever level they asked him to play, Cristiano Ronaldo dominated the game.

The dream of every young soccer player in Portugal is to be made part of the national team. This is the team that represents the country and competes in the European Championships as well as for the World Cup. It is the highest honor a soccer player could ask for.

No one from the small island of Madeira had ever played for Portugal's national team. By the time Cristiano was eleven, there was already a feeling that he could be the first. But he would need to leave the island of Madeira and play at one of the best academies in Portugal, Sporting FC, where the training and the competition would be better. The best club in Portugal's capital city of Lisbon flew the boy in for a tryout. He was so impressive that professional players stopped what they were doing to watch him train.

Privacy, Please

Cristiano Ronaldo, even today, remains a very private person. He is very close to his family but rarely talks about them. There have been many hurtful things written about his father's alcoholism and his brother's battle with drug addiction.

"I don't speak about my private life," Ronaldo said. "I simply don't speak about it."

They offered Cristiano a contract. His dream was coming true. But there would be some hard times ahead. He moved to Lisbon by himself, and he was homesick. He missed his mother. He also had a hard time adjusting to the way things were pronounced, causing him to have problems at school.

Cristiano became so unhappy that he wanted to quit soccer. The coaches at Sporting did not want an unhappy player,

> **"It was very difficult to face what I did at eleven. Leaving my family to go to the mainland was the worst moment of my life."**
>
> —Cristiano Ronaldo

so they sent Cristiano back home. He started playing soccer again for the local club, and his dream of becoming a soccer star seemed to be over. Again, fate, or his godfather Fernao Sousa, stepped in.

Sousa went and spoke to Cristiano. He urged him to give Lisbon another try. He told him that it would be a shame to waste the kind of soccer talent he had. He told him that Sporting FC was the best futbol club in all of Portugal. If they wanted him, then he must be great. Sousa also told him that if he continued with his soccer, he might one day be able to help his family and that his mother would no longer have to work two jobs just to feed her children.

In 2003, a baby-faced Cristiano Ronaldo signed a professional contract with English superteam Manchester United.

Cristiano was convinced, and he returned to Lisbon. There, he worked harder than anyone else and improved every year. He stayed after practice every day and trained for an extra hour. One of his teammates said that Cristiano wanted to make everyone who watched him play happy.

Cristiano stayed at the academy for the next several years, and by the time he was seventeen he was playing with the top team. But he wouldn't stay there long. One of the best teams in the world, Manchester United of the prestigious English Premier League, signed him to a contract immediately after playing an exhibition game, or a "friendly," against Sporting. Cristiano was only eighteen years old.

3

Dreams Come True

These days, Cristiano Ronaldo is known as one of the best soccer players in the world. He plays for Real Madrid, a top team in Spain's professional soccer league, known as La Liga. It is a treat for soccer fans to see him go head-to-head against Lionel "Leo" Messi, another soccer great, who plays for Real Madrid's rival: Barcelona.

Ronaldo dribbles the ball away from Lionel Messi. Ronaldo and Messi are often considered the two best players in the world.

"It's part of my life now. People are bound to compare us."
—Cristiano Ronaldo, on always being compared to Leo Messi

Playing for Manchester United in England between 2003 and 2009 made Ronaldo an international soccer star. But it was also during that time that he suffered the loss of his father, Dinis, who died from liver disease because of his alcoholism.

Seeing his father battle the demons of alcohol addiction for so long caused Ronaldo to swear that he would never drink alcohol in his life. It was a tough loss for the rising young soccer star. After all, despite his difficulties, Dinis would always be his son's biggest fan and supporter. In fact, before his son traveled to England, Dinis rarely missed a game.

"Those are most treasured memories," Dinis said during an interview. "Each time he played away, I had a place reserved for me on the bus or the plane."

When Ronaldo arrived at the headquarters for the famed English soccer club Manchester United, the team's manager asked him what number he would like to have. Since he was so used to wearing the number 28, that was the one he asked for. But the team's manager, Sir Alex Ferguson, laughed and gave Ronaldo a jersey with the number 7 on it.

Ronaldo's athleticism and drive set him apart.

Ronaldo immediately knew what that meant. Manchester United only gives out the number 7 to its best superstars. Ronaldo was given the number before he ever even played for them. Now he would follow in the footsteps of soccer legends like George Best and David Beckham, who wore the number before him. He knew it was an honor, and he knew he would have to work hard to make his new team proud. And work he did.

He scored his first English Premier League goal on November 1, 2003, during a 3–0 victory. He started earning more and more playing time and scored ten goals during the 2005–2006 season. Fans responded by voting him as the FIFPro Special Young Player of the Year. The following year, Ronaldo scored twenty-three goals. Then other teams from other leagues—like La Liga's Real Madrid—began thinking of ways to sign the young star away from Manchester United.

But there were other family problems to come. Ronaldo's mother developed cancer and became very sick. Having just lost his father only a few years earlier, Ronaldo was very worried. He traveled to Portugal whenever he could to be with his family. He couldn't stand the idea of losing his mother as well as his father.

Even though he was the youngest of four children, Ronaldo felt responsible for everyone else in his family. That was true now more than ever. Not only was he making more money than they ever dreamed but his older brother had become addicted to drugs. It was up to Ronaldo to try to keep his family together. And somehow, he would have to put all these personal problems aside and continue producing for Manchester United.

Ronaldo uses his leaping ability to head in a goal for Manchester United during a 2008 match against Chelsea.

And he did! Ronaldo produced some of the best soccer anyone had ever seen. He led Manchester United by scoring a whopping forty-two goals during the 2007–2008 season. When it came time to hand out the end-of-season awards, it seemed as if Cristiano Ronaldo would have to build a new room to hold all of his trophies.

During that off-season, Ronaldo basically won every award that soccer has to offer. He won the Ballon d'Or (given to the best player in Europe), the FIFA World Player of the Year, the FIFPro Player of the Year, the World Soccer Player of the Year, and the European Golden Shoe.

His mother eventually recovered, and to this day Ronaldo remains very close to his mother and sisters.

The Cristiano Ronaldo Scowl

It has been noted over the years that Cristiano Ronaldo always looks angry or upset when he is playing soccer. Sometimes he gets into arguments with players from opposing teams or complains to the referee. When he was asked about it, Ronaldo explained that it is only because of how much he hates to lose. Remember, this is the same player who was nicknamed "Crybaby" by his own teammates when he was playing in youth leagues.

"I agree that I have a bad image ... because I'm too serious," he said. "I hate to lose. I'm a competitive man and sometimes people interpret that in a different way."

During that special season, the world began to take notice of this great player. They started comparing him to some of the all-time great players. This was when Ronaldo's lifelong dream of being the first soccer player from the small island of Madeira to be named to Portugal's national team also came true.

He represented his country in several tournaments, but none is bigger than the FIFA World Cup. It is held only once every four years and features the best teams from across the globe. In 2006, Cristiano Ronaldo got a chance to play in his first World Cup matches.

He scored seven goals during the qualifying matches leading up to the World Cup and then scored a goal during the second game of the 2006 World Cup against the national team from Iran.

Even though he rose to fame at Manchester United and became a worldwide star, Ronaldo never really felt comfortable in England. Remember how he felt out of place trying to learn the different dialect in Lisbon as a young boy? This was worse. The English language was very hard to learn and the culture in England is much different from Portugal.

Ronaldo shoots and scores on this penalty kick during a 2006 World Cup match against Iran.

Ronaldo always had his eye on playing for Real Madrid, one of the top teams in Spain. The culture in Spain is very similar to that of Portugal, and the Spanish language is very close to Portuguese. Most people who speak one can understand the other. In 2009, Real Madrid offered Manchester United $130 million to sign Ronaldo away. And so the star set off to Spain.

What do you do when you score? Celebrate!

Ronaldo was able to fit in right away with his new club. In an amazing display of his skills, he scored thirty-three goals in only thirty-five games for Real Madrid that season! Incredibly he was able to top that the following year when he scored a whopping sixty times in fifty-five appearances—that's more than one goal per game.

4

Giving Back

Cristiano Ronaldo is one of the richest and most successful soccer players in history. He has amassed a fortune playing the game he loves so much. But he has also made a fortune through clothing and shoe lines named CR7. This also happens to be his nickname—using his initials and his jersey number.

> **"I'm living a dream I never want to wake up from."**
>
> —Cristiano Ronaldo

Ronaldo has never forgotten where he came from and the poverty that his family endured. He paid for a cancer center to be started in his hometown and also opened up a soccer museum there. However, his charitable work and philanthropy go much deeper.

Ronaldo was watching television in 2004 when something affected him deeply. It was just after Christmas Day when news aired of a terrible earthquake in the ocean that caused a giant tidal wave, or tsunami, in the Indian Ocean. The tsunami ravaged parts of Asia, especially the country of Indonesia. There, on the television, was the image of a little boy wearing a number 7 Cristiano Ronaldo jersey.

The boy's parents had been killed by the tidal wave, and he was homeless. He survived for more than two weeks by drinking water from puddles.

Moved by the tragedy of the 2004 Indonesian tsunami, Ronaldo traveled there to meet with a survivor who was wearing a Ronaldo jersey when he was rescued.

"This really got to me, after seeing the images I was really touched," Ronaldo told reporters. He decided he would visit Indonesia to see what he could do. He visited an area known as Banda Aceh, where he helped raise money for reconstruction of homes as well as care for the survivors. Miraculously, he was also able to track down the little boy he saw on television

The 2004 Tsunami

The worst national disaster many of us will ever see in our lifetimes occurred on December 26, 2004, shortly after a massive earthquake in the Indian Ocean off the coast of Sumatra, Indonesia. The quake caused the water to rise rapidly and become a giant tidal wave, or tsunami. Many countries were affected, including Indonesia, Thailand, and India. Nearly 300,000 people were killed and many bodies were never recovered as the water swept through villages and cities at a high speed.

wearing his jersey. The ten-year-old boy, named Martunis, was thrilled to meet his hero. Ronaldo spent time with him playing video games and, of course, soccer. He also helped the boy's surviving family personally with a donation of money and gave the boy several Manchester United soccer jerseys.

"When I met him in person and reflected on what he had gone through, it was rather difficult," Ronaldo told a television news reporter. "Over the time I spent in his company I noticed that he is quite a brave, beautiful and healthy boy."

The following year Ronaldo's own hometown was hit by a terrible flood and mudslides that killed more than forty people. Houses, schools, and medical offices were destroyed. Ronaldo responded immediately to help his hometown. He arranged for a charity soccer match to take place that would include his being on one of the teams. All the money raised from the game went to help pay for the island's recovery.

Though he is very private regarding his personal life, family, and charitable efforts, it was learned that Ronaldo routinely pays the bills of cancer patients in his hometown, especially the children. He has also helped raise and donated money to several other charitable organizations throughout the world. That makes Cristiano Ronaldo a true champion away from the soccer fields that have made him famous.

He has also continued to dominate the game and work hard at being a champion on the field. He remains the hardest worker on his team, whether he is dressing for Real Madrid or for Portugal's national team. He still regularly stays, even after all others have left the practice field, to continue striving to get better.

And while he is regarded as one of the best to ever play the game, that championship, especially for Portugal, continued to elude him. While Portugal is regarded as a top tier national team, it is usually not mentioned in the same conversations as the national teams from Spain, Germany, Italy, Brazil, France, or Argentina. Those are considered the elite teams in the world. For Portugal to win the World Cup or the European Championships, it would be considered an upset.

It's all about controlling the ball! Ronaldo puts in extra time during training to perfect his skills.

Ronaldo's international career has been impressive as he has scored more than fifty goals against the best teams the world has to offer during international matches. In 2014, he became the first player from Portugal to score goals in three different World Cup tournaments.

That almost didn't happen. Ronaldo suffered a serious leg injury just before the World Cup. He couldn't even practice with his teammates, twice having to be helped off the field during training sessions. Even though doctors warned that he could risk his career by continuing to play, Ronaldo said he could not let his countrymen down. He scored the decisive goal in a victory against Ghana and also assisted on a goal during a 2–2 draw with the United States. But the team was shut down by Germany 4–0 and was eliminated from play. Still, his country, his teammates, and the world saw how dedicated he was to his country's national team, and that only caused his legend to grow more.

Ronaldo uses his body to keep the ball from American defender Graham Zusi during a 2014 World Cup match against the United States.

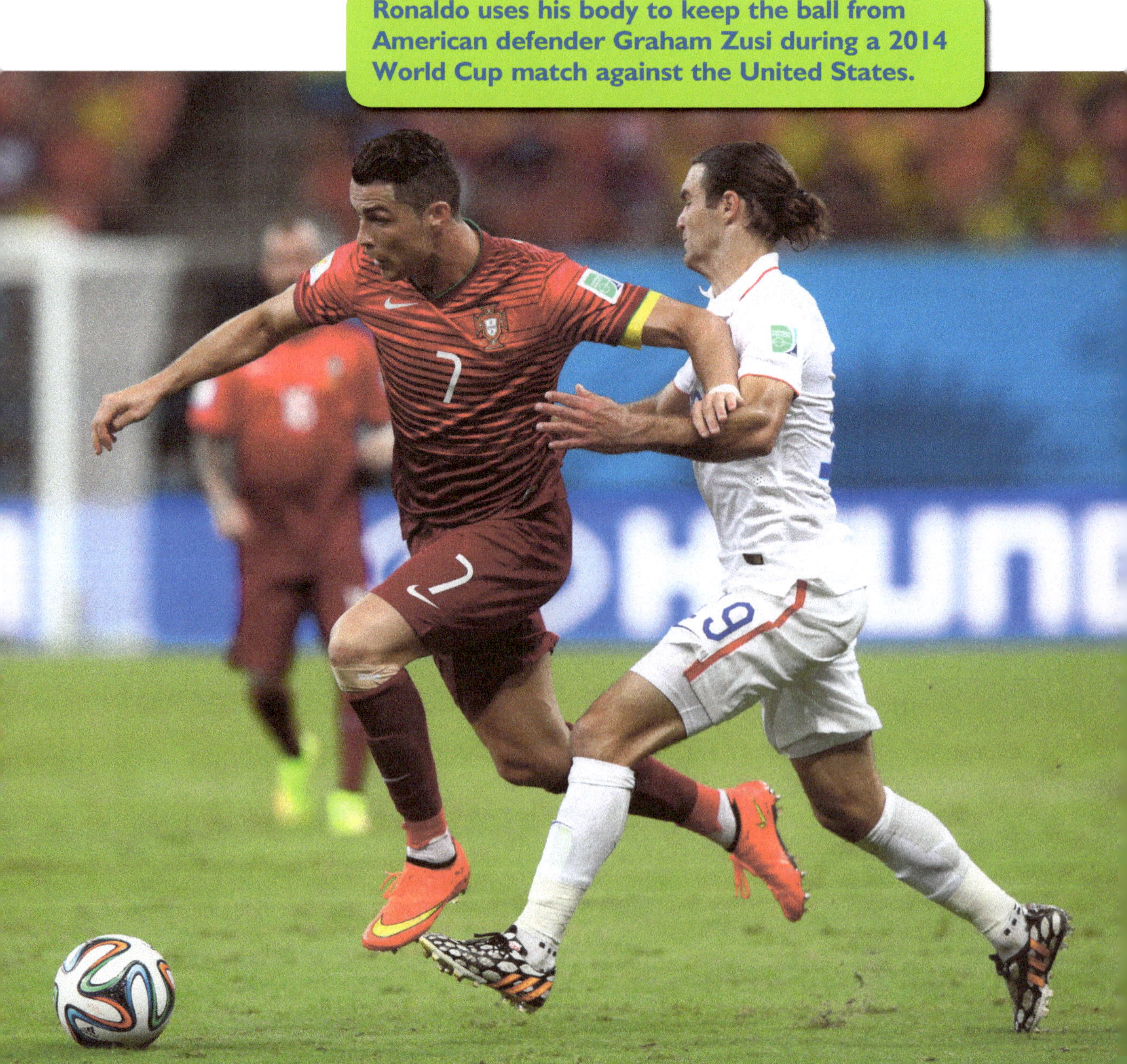

The stage was set for the summer of 2016: the European Championships. When Ronaldo scored three goals, or a hat trick, against Armenia in the European Championship qualifiers, it gave him twenty-three Euro goals, making him the all-time leading European Championship scorer.

Portugal advanced to the knockout stage, and when Ronaldo's shot bounced off Croatia's goalkeeper, it went right to another Portugal player who scored for the victory. The team then beat Poland on penalty kicks and was set to play upstart Wales in the semifinals. Ronaldo scored one goal and assisted on another to lead his team to the finals against a powerhouse French squad.

Now, only ninety minutes stood in the way of a championship for Cristiano Ronaldo and the Portuguese national team. His team was very confident because of the dominant way he was playing. Surely he would lead them to the trophy.

Then came the hard tackle only twenty-eight minutes into the match. Ronaldo cried in agony, clutching his knee. He tried twice to get back on the field. Finally the team's medical staff had to bring a stretcher onto the field and carry him off.

The team's mood darkened. How could they win without their best player? But a true champion does whatever it takes to help his team. That's when Ronaldo, the superstar

The sweet taste of victory. Ronaldo kisses the 2016 European Championship trophy after Portugal's 1–0 victory over France.

soccer player, became Ronaldo, the superstar coach and cheerleader, willing his team to win. Portugal shocked France with a late goal.

It was the first international championship ever won by Portugal in soccer.

Ronaldo was now a champion.

5

Global Sensation

Cristiano Ronaldo was now a champion in the truest sense of the word. He was also a global sensation. How do you top winning a European Championship for your country?

How about making 2016 the sixth consecutive season to score more than fifty goals? Or, how about signing a new contract with Real Madrid to become not only the highest paid player in soccer but ensuring continued play for Madrid until 2021?

And why shouldn't Madrid reward its best player? After all, in a little more than six seasons Ronaldo has scored an amazing 372 goals in 360 matches! He has also led Real Madrid to two Champions League titles, two Copas del Rey, and one La Liga title.

Ronaldo happily announces his new contract with Real Madrid in 2016.

There really isn't much left for the young superstar to prove. He was very happy to earn the new contract but said it would not be his last. He promised to continue playing the game for as long as he loves it and for as long as it is fun.

"This is a special day for me, to continue this link with the club of my heart, it is a unique moment for me," Ronaldo said. "[But] it is not my last contract. My aim for these five years is to keep making history, giving my best for this jersey. For sure I will do the same as before, give everything to win trophies, and score goals."

It truly has been a remarkable ride for the kid from the poor neighborhood on the small island. The odds were truly against him. He overcame the challenges associated with poverty and a father addicted to alcohol. Now he is a household name in many parts of the world.

Ronaldo has made numerous magazine headlines for his choice in girlfriends. He normally dates the top supermodels in the world and is seen at the biggest social events throughout the world with them. Ronaldo is also routinely named as one of the best-looking men in the world, and his fashion sense and style often land him in the latest fashion magazines. He has been hired to be a spokesman for numerous clothing designers, health and fitness specialists, hair gels, and men's fragrances.

He has recently expanded his CR7 clothing line to include more items, such as premium shirts and shoes that are available in exclusive department stores.

Ronaldo loves collecting fast cars and lives in lavish homes. He recently purchased an apartment worth millions of dollars in New York's Trump Tower, even though he is rarely in New York.

Cristiano Ronaldo models a new style of shoes from his FW15 CR7 Footwear collection.

Ronaldo also remains very involved in numerous children's charities, especially Save the Children.

Despite his public appearances and flair, he also stays extremely private about his personal life. It may seem like a contradiction, but he never speaks about his family. It was learned that he purchased his mother a large house in Portugal, and he also bought houses for each of his two sisters.

> **"I often feel misunderstood. I am a very private person and am down-to-earth."**
> —Cristiano Ronaldo

In 2010, Ronaldo did announce the birth of his son in the United States. But the only thing he ever said about Cristiano Ronaldo Jr. was that he has full custody. He has never revealed who the boy's mother is, though he has indicated that he would like more children. He said his son comes to every single one of his matches and cheers him on.

"[Being a father] changed everything ... it's unbelievable, it's a great feeling," he told a British newspaper. "My friends ask me if I want more kids and I always say yes, I want more, it's the best thing you can have in your life."

Despite all the success off the field, Ronaldo knows that his legacy will be remembered only for one thing: being a

Ronaldo poses with his son, Cristiano Ronaldo Jr., and mother, Maria Dolores Aveiro, at the premiere of a documentary of his life.

great soccer player. And it is that desire to not only succeed but also to be great or even the greatest that drives him to work so hard.

"Talent without working hard is nothing," Ronaldo said. "Every season is a new challenge to me and I always set out to improve."

Ronaldo's incredible 2016 season catapulted him to win the annual FIFA Ballon d'Or—or "Golden Ball"—awarded every year to the best soccer player in the world. Ronaldo had already taken home the award in 2008, 2013, and 2014. His rival, Leo Messi, who plays for Barcelona, has won the award a record five times.

Upon winning his fourth time in 2016, Ronaldo said, "For me it's an unbelievable moment, I'm so proud, so happy.

Thank you to everyone who voted for me. Thank you to my teammates … Portugal national team, and this trophy's for Real Madrid."

Messi vs. Ronaldo

For the last ten years, soccer fans have been arguing back and forth: Who is the better player, Leo Messi or Cristiano Ronaldo?

The truth is you can't go wrong choosing either. It is also true that they are vastly different players. Yes, both players excite fans with their speed and ferocity and amazing goals, but Cristiano Ronaldo is built more like the prototypical striker. This is the player that tries to get as forward as he can in front of the goal to try and score. He is tall and can use his head to flick the ball past the keeper.

Messi, nicknamed "the flea" because he is shorter than just about everyone else on the soccer field, is more of a playmaker. As an attacking midfielder, his job is to try and create scoring opportunities not only for himself but for his teammates as well.

Ronaldo poses with teammates and his 2013 Ballon d'Or trophy, given to the best player in Europe.

Hunger, determination, and drive set players like Cristiano Ronaldo apart from others. It is that desire that perhaps causes his critics to complain about his attitude or anger on the field of play. But it is that same desire that will certainly enthrall soccer fans for years to come as we continue to witness one of the greatest athletes of all time.

"I want more and more, I still have many years to play football, and I want to win more things," Ronaldo said. "I'm always motivated."

Stats, Honors, and Records

CLUB STATISTICS													
CLUB	SEASON			CUP		LEAGUE CUP		EUROPE		OTHER		TOTAL	
		Apps	Goals	Apps	Goals	Apps	Goals	Apps	Goals	Apps	Goals	Apps	Goals
Sporting CP B	2002–03	2	0	—		—		—		—		2	0
Sporting CP	2002–03	25	3	3	2	—		3	0	0	0	31	5
Manchester United	2003–04	29	4	5	2	1	0	5	0	0	0	40	6
	2004–05	33	5	7	4	2	0	8	0	0	0	50	9
	2005–06	33	9	2	0	4	2	8	1	—		47	12
	2006–07	34	17	7	3	1	0	11	3	—		53	23
	2007–08	34	31	3	3	0	0	11	8	1	0	49	42
	2008–09	33	18	2	1	4	2	12	4	2	1	53	26
	Total	196	84	26	13	12	4	55	16	3	1	292	118
Real Madrid	2009–10	29	26	0	0	—		6	7	—		35	33
	2010–11	34	40	8	7	—		12	6	—		54	53
	2011–12	38	46	5	3	—		10	10	2	1	55	60
	2012–13	34	34	7	7	—		12	12	2	2	55	55
	2013–14	30	31	6	3	—		11	17	—		47	51
	2014–15	35	48	2	1	—		12	10	5	2	54	61
	2015–16	36	35	0	0	—		12	16	—		48	51
	Total	236	260	28	21	—		75	78	9	5	348	364
Career total		459	347	57	36	12	4	133	94	12	6	673	487

NATIONAL TEAM	YEAR	APPS	GOALS	RATIO
Portugal	2003	2	0	0.00
	2004	16	7	0.44
	2005	11	2	0.18
	2006	14	6	0.43
	2007	10	5	0.50
	2008	8	1	0.13
	2009	7	1	0.14

NATIONAL TEAM	YEAR	APPS	GOALS	RATIO
Portugal (continued)	2010	11	3	0.27
	2011	8	7	0.88
	2012	13	5	0.38
	2013	9	10	1.11
	2014	9	5	0.56
	2015	5	3	0.60
	2016	13	13	1.00
Total		136	68	0.50

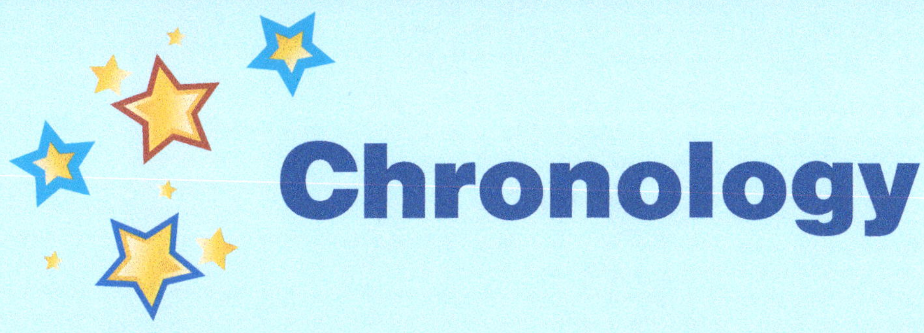

Chronology

1985 Cristiano Ronaldo dos Santos Aveiro is born on February 5.

1993 Starts playing in an organized soccer league.

1995 Joins Nacional.

1997 Makes big decision to play for Sporting in Lisbon, away from family.

2003–2004 Transfers to Manchester United.

2005 Voted special young player of the year.

2005 Father passes away.

2006 Leads Portugal to fourth-place finish in the World Cup.

2007–2008 Wins the Premier League Golden Boot; wins first Ballon d'Or.

2009 Transfers to Real Madrid.

2010 Is voted World Cup Man of the Match.

2010 Son is born.

2013 Wins Ballon d'Or.

2014 Wins Ballon d'Or.

2016 Leads Portugal to European Championship; wins Ballon d'Or.

Glossary

adept Skilled at something.

amassed Collected in large numbers.

appearance In soccer, actively participating in a match.

Ballon d'Or The "Golden Ball" award given annually to the best player in soccer.

cultivate To help grow or get better.

improbable Very unlikely.

La Liga The official professional soccer league in Spain.

motivational Inspiring someone to do better.

obsession Something upon which one solely concentrates.

philanthropy Doing charitable work and donating money to help the less fortunate.

prestigious Something worthy of being admired.

spokesman A person who represents a group or a company.

striker In soccer, the player who plays closest to the other team's goal and tries to score.

tsunami A giant ocean wave, often caused by an earthquake.

Further Reading

Books

Logothetis, Paul. *Cristiano Ronaldo: International Soccer Star.* Edina, MN: ABDO Publishing, 2015.

Spragg, Iain. *Cristiano Ronaldo: Ultimate Fan Book.* London, UK: Carlton Books, 2017.

Torres, John A. *Soccer Star Cristiano Ronaldo—Goal! Latin Stars of Soccer.* New York: Enslow Publishers, Inc., 2014.

Websites

Cristiano Ronaldo Official Site
cristianoronaldo.com
An official fan site featuring statistics, a timeline, and feature stories.

ESPN FC
espnfc.us/player/22774/cristiano-ronaldo
News, statistics, and analysis of Cristiano Ronaldo.

Index